MICHAEL BOND
Paddington
takes a BATH
Illustrated by Barry Wilkinson

COLLINS COLOUR CUBS

Mr. and Mrs. Brown first met Paddington on a railway platform, which was how he came to have such an unusual name for a bear, because Paddington was the name of the station.

When they discovered he'd come all the way from Darkest Peru and had nowhere to go, they decided to take him home with them, and while Mrs. Brown went to look for their daughter, Judy, Mr. Brown took him to the refreshment room.

Paddington had never been in a station
buffet before and he soon got in a mess.

Even the taxi driver had second thoughts when he saw the state Paddington was in.

"Bears is sixpence extra," he exclaimed. "*Sticky* bears is ninepence!"

But at long last they arrived at Number
Thirty-two Windsor Gardens, where the
Brown family lived.

"Now you are going to meet Mrs. Bird," said Judy. "She's a bit fierce sometimes, but I'm sure you'll like her."

"I'm sure I shall if you say so," said Paddington. "The thing is . . . will she like *me*?"

The door was opened by a stout, mother-ly lady with a kindly twinkle in her eye.

"Goodness gracious!" she exclaimed when she saw Paddington. "Whatever have you got there?"

"It's not a *what*," said Judy. "It's a bear. His name's Paddington and he's coming to stay with us."

"Mercy me!" cried Mrs. Bird. "I haven't put clean sheets in the spare room or anything – though judging by the state he's in perhaps that's just as well! I think he'd better have a bath straight away."

"I've had an accident with a cream bun, Mrs. Bird," said Paddington, as Judy led him upstairs for a bath.

"Where did you say you came from?" called Mrs. Bird.

"Darkest Peru," replied Paddington.

"Hmm!" said Mrs. Bird. "Then I expect you like marmalade. I'd better get some extra supplies in."

"Fancy her knowing I like marmalade,"
said Paddington, as Judy led the way
towards the bathroom.

"Mrs. Bird knows · everything about
everything," said Judy's brother, Jonathan.

While Jonathan got the bath ready,
Judy explained matters to Paddington.

"There's one tap marked hot," she said, "and one marked cold. Here's a cake of soap and a clean towel. Oh, and there's a brush, so that you can scrub your back."

"It sounds very complicated," said Paddington. "Couldn't I just sit in a puddle?"

"I don't think Mrs. Bird would approve
of that," said Judy. "And don't forget to
wash your ears. They look awfully black."

"They're meant to be black!" exclaimed Paddington hotly. " . . . I think."

After Jonathan and Judy had left, Paddington peered at his ears in the mirror. He decided that perhaps they were rather black after all.

Luckily, there was a tube of white stuff on the washbasin, so he was soon able to put them right again.

After that, Paddington tried writing his name on the mirror, but it was much longer than he'd expected and he soon ran out of tooth paste.

He was beginning to feel hungry again, but the cake of soap Judy had given him didn't taste like any sort of cake he'd ever eaten before. In fact, it made him feel rather sick.

Unaware of the problems Paddington was having, Jonathan and Judy got ready for tea in the room below.

"I do wish Paddington could stay for good," said Judy. "He's all alone, and London is such a big place if you have nowhere to go."

"I daresay," said Mr. Brown, "but I still think we ought to report the matter to someone. Anyway," he added darkly, "it all depends on Mrs. Bird."

Just then the door opened and Mrs. Bird herself came in. Everyone went very quiet as they waited to see what she had to say.

"I suppose you want to tell me you've decided to keep that young bear?" she said. "I must say I'm very pleased. He raised his hat, and I like bears with good manners."

"Fancy that!" said Mrs. Brown, after Mrs. Bird had gone. "Whoever would have thought when we left home this morning that we'd end up having a bear living with us!"

"Hooray!" said Judy. "I can't wait to tell Paddington. Just as soon as he's finished his bath. . . ."

But far from finishing his bath, Paddington hadn't even started yet. He was too busy drawing a map of Darkest Peru on the bathroom floor with some of Mr. Brown's shaving cream.

In fact, he was so busy, it wasn't until
he felt a trickle of water run down the
back of his neck that he realised the bath
was full of foaming water.

He tried looking for the taps, but he couldn't find them anywhere.

And when he stood up again, he couldn't see the bathroom either!

In the end he decided there was only
one thing for it — that was to jump in!

But he soon discovered it's one thing
jumping into a bath . . .

. . . but it's quite another matter getting out again, especially when the sides are slippery and your eyes are full of soap. He tried bailing out the water with his hat.

Then he called out "Help!" – at first in quite a quiet voice so that he wouldn't disturb anyone, then in a much louder voice. "HELP! HELP!"

"That's funny," said Mr. Brown, "I could have sworn I felt a spot of water."

"So did I," said Jonathan.

Judy jumped to her feet, pulling Jonathan after her. "Come on!" she hissed.

"What's up?" asked Jonathan.

"It must be to do with Paddington," whispered Judy. "I bet he's in trouble again."

"Are you all right, Paddington?"
called Judy.

"No!" cried Paddington, "I'm not! I think I may be going to drown."

"Gosh!" said Jonathan, when he saw the state the bathroom was in. "What a mess! Even I've never made a mess like this."

"Oh, Paddington!" said Judy, as she and Jonathan helped him out of the bath. "Thank goodness you're all right. I should never have forgiven myself if anything had happened to you."

"It's a good job I was wearing my hat," said Paddington.

"Why on earth didn't you pull the plug out?" asked Jonathan.

"Nobody said anything about that," said Paddington. "I wish I really had sat in a puddle now. I shall never, ever, have a proper bath again."

All the same, when Paddington came downstairs again everyone had to admit that he was looking much, much cleaner than when they had first met him.

Mrs. Bird brought in a fresh pot of tea
and a large pile of marmalade sandwiches,
and in no time at all things were back
to normal.

But before he went to bed that night Paddington had one more go at having a bath, only this time he made sure the taps were turned off.

"It's what's known as a *dry* bath," he
announced. "It's safer than using water,
and it's much less messy."

*This story comes from A BEAR CALLED PADDINGTON
and is based on the television film. It has
been specially written by Michael Bond
for younger children.*

ISBN 0 00 123335 1 (paperback)
ISBN 0 00 123340 8 (cased)
Text Copyright © 1976 Michael Bond
Illustrations Copyright © 1976 William Collins Sons & Co. Ltd.
Cover Copyright © 1976 William Collins Sons & Co. Ltd. and FilmFair Ltd.
Cover design by Ivor Wood. Cover photographed by Bruce Scott.

Printed in Great Britain